Walt Disney's

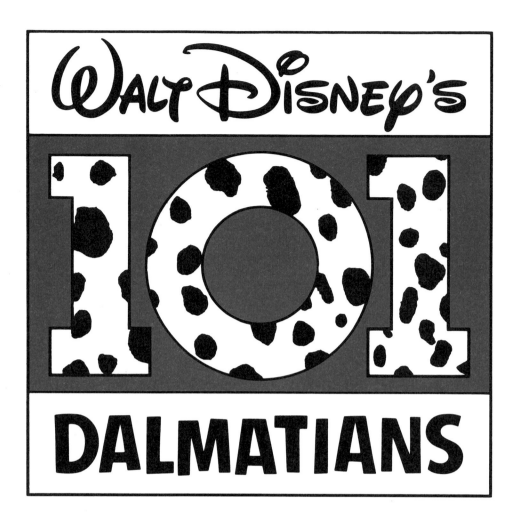

101 DALMATIANS

ADAPTED FROM THE FILM BY

ANN BRAYBROOKS

ILLUSTRATED BY

GIL DiCICCO

DISNEY
PRESS
NEW YORK

My story begins in London, not so very long ago. Yet so much has happened since then, it seems like an eternity.

At that time, I lived with my pet in a bachelor flat, just off Regent's Park. It was a beautiful spring day, a boring time for bachelors. As usual, my pet preferred to stay indoors and work at his piano, for he was a musician of sorts. Roger Radcliff hadn't sold a single song yet, but I still had hope for the old boy.

I'd been living with Roger for a while, and as far as I could see, the old notion that a bachelor's life was so much fun was all nonsense. It was downright dull. My pet needed someone, but if it were left to Roger, we'd be bachelors forever. He was married to his work, and he spent all his time writing songs about love: a subject he knew nothing about.

Roger is smart enough, as humans go. As for his looks, it's true that he doesn't have a smooth coat and spots, as I do. Yet I'd been comparing him to the people I saw on television, and it seemed to me that Roger was a rather handsome animal in his way. Certainly, any dog would be proud to have his strong jaw and nose, and to be so tall and thin.

I could see no reason why my pet didn't deserve an attractive wife, and I was determined to do my best to help him. Of course, a dog is a pretty poor judge of human beauty, but I'd seen enough fashion magazines to give me a rough idea.

While Roger tootled away at the piano, I rested my head on the windowsill, watching the passersby below. I kept an eye out for four legs and two . . . that is, for a dog and her pet.

On this particular spring day, I saw an Afghan hound slink down the sidewalk. Her pet had long, stringy hair and a proud nose, and stepped right behind her. What a strange pair! Definitely not for me and Roger.

Then I saw a rather short lady and her pug waddle by. Nope! I knew they weren't right.

Aha! I said to myself when I spied a French poodle and her pet. *Now there's a fancy breed!* I looked again and saw both their noses

pointed in the air. Perhaps they were just a bit *too* fancy.

A plump woman rode by on her bike, with a Pekingese propped in the basket. They were too old. And the next pair—a girl and her puppy—were too young.

I settled my head back on the windowsill. My eyes were just about to close when I saw her—the most beautiful creature on four legs! She had a straight, pointed tail and the most magnificent spots! I was afraid to look at her pet, lest I be disappointed. I wasn't. The woman behind her was just as lovely.

It was almost too good to be true. I knew I'd never find another pair like that if I looked for a hundred years. I saw them heading for

the park, the perfect meeting place. Somehow, I would have to get Roger out of the house. It would be difficult, because he never stopped work until five.

I moved quickly yet quietly. Although Roger's back was to me, I tiptoed behind him. I went up to the clock and very carefully moved one hand forward with my nose. Then I grabbed my leash in my mouth and ran to the front door. My barking surprised him.

"It's too early for your walk, Pongo!" he called to me from his seat at the piano. I jumped up on my hind legs and, front paws against the door, barked even louder.

From where I stood, I could see Roger check his watch, then look at the clock. "Oh, after five already," he said. "Fancy that." Poor

man! He thought his watch had stopped.

I scratched at the door and barked again, hoping to hurry him. "All right, Pongo," he said. "All right, boy. We'll go to the park."

I wagged my tail furiously. As soon as Roger opened the door, I yanked him out of the flat and down the sidewalk. He pulled on my leash, saying, "Pongo, old boy, take it easy! What's the rush?"

At the park, I hurried him past the fat lady and her pug. I made sure he didn't look at the creature with the Afghan. But as I dragged him down one path after another, I began to be afraid that we'd missed the lovely pair. Then I spotted them. The woman was sitting on a bench, reading a book. Her Dalmatian sat beside her.

I gazed up at Roger, who was looking the other way. That Roger!

He would settle down on the grass and puff his pipe, and that would be that. So I marched Roger right past the woman and her dog, both of whom lifted their eyes to look at us for a second.

Then Roger did just as I feared. He sat on the grass beside the pond, staring off into the distance! I was desperate. I needed to think of something, anything to attract attention. I jumped on Roger's back and snatched the hat off his head.

"Pongo!" he cried, trying to grab the hat. "You silly old thing. Come on, let me have my hat back!"

I didn't care how angry Roger became, I had to do something. I bounded over to the bench and set the hat on it. The woman looked up from her book, glancing at Roger.

For a moment, I thought my plan had worked. At least they had seen one another. I turned to grin at Roger, then looked back at the bench. For some strange reason, the pair had left.

At that moment, Roger grabbed me by the collar. As he snapped on my leash, he said, "Come on, you old rebel. We're going home."

I refused to give up. With Roger tugging on my leash, I ran down the path after the woman. As soon as we caught up, I wrapped my leash around her legs. Then I wound it around her and Roger, pulling them together.

"I beg your pardon!" cried Roger, trying to maintain his balance and tip his hat at the same time. "I'm so sorry, Miss. Please excuse me. I . . . I . . ."

"Well, I must say!" replied the woman, attempting to untangle herself. "What on earth!"

As they stumbled about, joined at the knees by my leash, they headed closer to the pond. The beautiful Dalmatian grabbed her pet's jacket in her teeth, but the cloth ripped and the woman tumbled into the water. Roger fell in after her. At that point, he let go of my leash!

When the woman sat up, she didn't look too pleased. Water streamed down her face as she exclaimed, "Just look at my new spring suit! And where's my new hat?"

Afraid of what I had done, I jumped in and grabbed her hat out of the water. I waited patiently as Roger helped her up, but I could tell that he was quite cross with me. Roger snatched the hat out of my mouth and handed it to the woman. "I'm so terribly sorry," he said to her. "I don't know what's come over him. He's never acted this way before."

"Never mind, never mind," she said, sniffling. "Please, just go away. You've done enough."

I looked at Roger, hoping that he would say something to cheer her up. When he didn't, I realized that I might have ruined our only chance at happiness.

2

Fortunately, happiness was not entirely out of our reach, thanks to a kindhearted mistake made by Roger.

As the woman stood by the pond, she pulled out a handkerchief to dry her eyes. When Roger noticed that it was sopping wet, he fished in his pocket and handed her his own. "Here, take mine," he said. If he had looked at the handkerchief, he would have realized that it was as drenched as hers!

I cringed when I saw her stare at his offering. But instead of being angry, she laughed out loud. When Roger looked at the handkerchief, he began to laugh too.

While they were laughing together, I glanced over at the four-legged creature. For the first time, she smiled at me. I grinned back, happy that I had been brash enough to drag her pet into the water.

It was only a matter of time before they became our brides. My vows to Perdita, and Roger's to Anita, took place the following spring.

For the first six months or so, we lived in a small house near the park. It was a modest little place, but just right for two couples starting out.

Now a second head joined mine at the windowsill, as Perdita and I watched the world pass by together. We saw many of the pairs that I used to see, and many new ones, too.

One afternoon I noticed that Perdita was sighing a lot as she watched the nannies stroll by with their prams. Since she had been feeling tired lately, I asked, "Perdita, darling, are you all right?"

"Of course, dear," she said, smiling gently. "After all, dogs were having puppies long before our time."

When I saw the look on her face, I knew it. I was going to be a father! I nuzzled Perdita on the cheek and then ran around the house, barking and carrying on like crazy.

The weeks passed quickly. In that time, Roger and Anita hired Nanny, a delightful old woman who doted on us. She was also a wonderful cook and housekeeper, but the way she went about her business, getting in tight corners with her broom and sliding under tables to retrieve napkins, made her seem almost canine. Perdita and I adored her as much as she loved us, and I knew Nanny would be a great comfort once the puppies arrived.

One night, as Perdita and I rested our heads on the windowsill, we heard a horn blaring as it approached our house. Perdita recognized the car before I did. "Oh, Pongo," she said, shivering. "It's her! It's that devil woman!"

Perdita used strong language only when the situation called for it. And there was only one creature who deserved such a harsh description. From the window, we saw a roadster skid around the corner, and out came the devil woman herself, Cruella De Vil.

Cruella was one of Anita's schoolmates, and she breezed in whenever she wanted something. On this particular night, Anita asked Nanny to let her in. Perdita rushed to the kitchen and hid herself under the stove. Roger wasn't too fond of Cruella himself, so he retreated to the attic and his music.

Before Nanny had a chance to get the door, Cruella flung it open herself. Cruella stalked into the room, and once again, I was reminded how much she resembled a mongrel who fancied herself a purebred. She tossed back her frightful mane of hair as she spoke to Anita.

"Darling, how are you?" cried Cruella without waiting for an answer. "I'm miserable, darling, as usual—perfectly wretched. Where are they? Where are they?"

As Cruella paced the room, she waved a long cigarette holder, leaving a trail of smoke drifting behind her. I sneezed violently as Anita politely waved her hand in front of her face. Anita never had a chance to answer Cruella, because her classmate headed toward the kitchen, talking all the while. "For heaven's sake, Anita, where are they?"

Raising an eyebrow, Anita asked, "Who, Cruella? I don't know who you mean."

"The puppies. The puppies!" screamed Cruella as she marched back into the room. "This is no time for games. Where are the little brutes?"

I retreated behind a chair, protecting both myself and Cruella. If she continued to speak like that about my family, I was afraid of what I would do to her.

Anita finally answered. "It'll be at least three weeks. No rushing these things, you know."

"Anita, you're such a wit!" Cruella laughed; then she turned toward me and beckoned with one of her long, bony fingers. "Here, dog. Here."

I backed farther behind the chair to avoid her. Fortunately, Anita diverted her attention. "Isn't that a new fur coat, Cruella?" she asked.

"It's my only true love, darling," replied Cruella, hugging her coat and grinning. "I live for furs. I worship furs. After all, is there a woman in all this wretched world who doesn't?"

Anita sat down at a table, thinking. "But there are so many other things we need. . . ."

"Sweet, simple Anita," sneered Cruella, waving her arms. "This little house is your dream castle. And poor Roger—he's your bold and fearless Sir Galahad."

I couldn't understand why Anita didn't respond to her classmate's vicious remarks. She let Cruella ramble on and on and light one cigarette after another, fouling the house with her evil words and smoke. I was relieved that Cruella didn't stub out a cigarette on the

photograph of me and Perdita, which she was examining closely. "And then, of course, you have your little spotted friends," she said, standing in front of the mantel. "I must say, they have perfectly beautiful coats."

"Won't you have some tea, Cruella?" Anita asked, reaching for the kettle.

Cruella whirled around and hurried toward the front door. "No, I've got to run, darling. Let me know when the puppies arrive. You will, won't you, dear?"

"Yes, Cruella," sighed Anita as she watched Cruella leave with a swish of her long fur coat.

A moment later, Cruella popped her head around the door. "Now, don't forget, Anita. It's a promise. See you in three weeks. Cheerio!" Then she slammed the door behind her.

3

After Cruella's visit, Perdita spent a lot of time resting in the kitchen. I'll never forget the look on Perdita's face when I tried to get her out from her hiding place under the stove. She gazed up at me sadly and said, "That witch! That devil woman wants our puppies! That's all she's after."

I tried to console her. "Don't worry, Perdy. Anita and Roger are onto her. Nothing's going to happen to our puppies."

Perdita was almost in tears. "But what does she want with them?" she asked. "She can't possibly love them, or want to take care of them." Perdy laid her head on the floor and closed her eyes. I felt truly sorry for her, but there was nothing I could do.

Perdita's spirits picked up on the day she was to give birth. When she was ready to deliver, I waited outside the room with Roger. Inside, Perdy was being cared for by Anita and Nanny.

As the night wore on, Roger and I watched the clock. I wished that I could move the hands forward, just as I had done on that glorious spring day. Nanny had promised to give us the news as soon as the first puppy was born, but it seemed as though we had been waiting for hours. I cocked my ear toward the door, desperately listening for the joyful yelps of newborn pups.

I heard the excited voice of Nanny. "The puppies are here!" she cried, appearing at the doorway.

"How . . . how many?" Roger asked.

"Eight!"

"Eight?" answered Roger, delighted. He scratched the top of my head. "By George, Pongo, eight puppies!" I barked happily, and Roger and I danced in circles together.

Nanny appeared at the door again. "Ten!"

"Eleven!" called Anita from inside the room.

Roger shook my paw, saying, "Eleven puppies, Pongo, old boy."

"Wait a minute, now," said Nanny, with just her hand waving from the doorway. "Thirteen. No, no—fourteen. Oh, fifteen! Fifteen!"

Before I could faint, Nanny appeared and rubbed my nose. "And the mother's doing fine, love," she said, hugging me.

Nanny bustled back into the other room to check on the puppies. Roger cupped my head in his hands. "Fifteen puppies!" he exclaimed, looking me in the eye. "Why, Pongo, boy, that's marvelous! Why, you old rascal!"

I heard Nanny's footsteps behind me and whirled around, half expecting her to say that the number of puppies had risen to sixteen. Instead, she handed a small cloth bundle to Roger. "Four—fourteen," she managed to say, trying not to let us see her cry. "We lost one, the poor little thing."

I lowered my eyes. When Roger saw how sad I was, he stroked my ears. "Oh, Pongo, boy," he said, "it's just one of those things. And yet . . . and yet, I wonder . . ."

Puzzled, I looked up. Roger was rubbing the tiny body wrapped in the cloth. I assumed that he was trying to get its heart beating. He rubbed and rubbed, and nothing happened. Then I saw it. The cloth began to move under Roger's hands. "Look, Pongo! Look!" cried Roger as a small head emerged, then rested on Roger's hand.

"Anita! Nanny!" yelled Roger happily. "Fifteen! We still have fifteen!"

I gratefully licked Roger's face. Anita and Nanny hurried into the room, and Roger held out the puppy to show them. "See?" Roger said. "He's as good as new."

As we all gazed at the puppy, Anita couldn't help but repeat, "Fifteen puppies. Can you imagine that? Fifteen!"

Before she could say it again, thunder cracked outside. Startled, we looked up to see Cruella at the doorway. She swooped into the room, her long fur coat trailing behind her.

"Fifteen puppies!" she cried, advancing toward us. "How marvelous! How perfectly marvelous!" Reaching down, she tore away the cloth that covered the puppy. "Ugh!" she groaned. "Oh, the devil take it, they're mongrels! They don't have any spots—no spots at all! What a horrid little white rat! Ugh!"

Nanny bristled. "They're not mongrels," she explained. "They're always born like this. They'll get their spots. Just wait and see!"

"That's right, Cruella," added Anita calmly. "They'll have their spots in a few weeks."

Cruella's mouth twisted into a grin. "In that case, I'll take them all," she stated, pulling out her checkbook. "The whole litter. Just name your price, Anita."

"I'm afraid we can't give them up," she replied. "Poor Perdita would be heartbroken."

"Anita, don't be ridiculous! You can't possibly afford to keep them. You can scarcely afford to feed yourselves."

· 32 ·

"I'm sure we'll manage," Anita said, looking over at Roger.

Cruella sneered. "Yes, yes, I know—Roger's songs. Roger will sell one of his songs! Now, really, enough of this nonsense." Cruella sat at the desk and began writing out a check. "I'll pay you twice what they're worth. Come now, I'm being more than generous."

As Cruella fiddled with the pen, Roger and I became angrier and angrier. When she asked how soon the puppies could leave their mother, my lips curled back in a snarl. Roger crossed his arms and pronounced, "Never! The puppies will never leave this house."

Cruella leaped up from her chair, hovering over Roger. "What?" she yelled. "What did you say?"

Roger leaned backward but kept his feet planted on the floor. "I said we're . . . we're not . . . selling the puppies. Not . . . not a single one! Do you understand?"

Cruella glanced at Anita in disbelief. "Is he serious?" she asked. "Surely he must be joking!"

Roger glared at Cruella, shaking his head. "No, no . . . I mean it," he stated. "No, you're not getting one. Not one! And . . . and that's final!"

Cruella stomped around the room. "All right, keep the little beasts for all I care!" she screeched. "Do as you like with them. Drown them! But I warn you, I'll get even. Just wait—you'll be sorry. You fools! You—you idiots!"

She stormed out of the house. For the time being, the puppies were safe.

4

The first few weeks with the puppies brought me and Perdita nothing but joy. As the puppies got their spots, it became difficult at times to know who was who!

We had Patch and Pepper, who liked to balance on Perdy's back whenever she lay down. There was Penny, who stuck close to me. Rolly was quite a handful. Our roly-poly pup was always begging Perdita for more food. "I'm hungry, Mother," Rolly would whine. "I'm hungry."

"Now, Rolly," Perdita would say, "you just had your dinner."

"But I'm hungry, just the same," Rolly answered, and more than once, he added, "I'm so hungry, I could eat a . . . a whole elephant!"

As much as Rolly loved to eat, Lucky adored watching television. Whenever the family gathered in front of the set, Lucky would jump up and put his little paws at the bottom of the screen, blocking everyone's view!

"Get down, Lucky!" the other puppies would shout. "We can't see. Mother, make him get down." And Perdita would have to ask Lucky to sit down.

At night, it was difficult to tear the puppies away from the set, even after the program was over and the commercials came on. On one particular evening, I wish that we had stayed up with them, instead of shepherding them off to bed so Perdy and I could take our walk.

As usual, we left the puppies with Nanny. While we were strolling in the park with Roger and Anita, she received quite a fright, and our whole world was turned upside down.

The trouble started when Nanny was putting the puppies to bed in the kitchen. The doorbell rang, and she hurried to open it. Standing on the porch was a tall, skinny man wearing a turtleneck pulled up to his mouth and a beret yanked down to his eyebrows. Beside him was a shorter, fatter fellow dressed the same way.

"Good evening, mum," said the skinny one, Jasper. "We're here to inspect the . . . ah, the wirin' and switches."

"We're from the gas company," added the fat one, Horace.

"Electric company!" Jasper corrected him. "Electric!"

Nanny looked at one, then the other. She kept the door partly closed behind her as she replied, "But we didn't call for any inspection."

Jasper coughed, then continued. "Ah, yes, mum, I know. You see, there's a new act that's just been passed in Parliament. Comes under the heading of Defense of the Realm. It's number 104, section 29. It's very important. It's the law." When he could see that Nanny wasn't falling for it, he added, "And it's for your own safety, mum."

"I don't care what Parliament or anyone says," shouted Nanny. "You're not comin' in here! Not with the mister and missus gone."

Nanny tried to shut the door, but Jasper pushed against it and almost toppled her over. "We got no time to talk," insisted Jasper, bursting into the house with Horace behind him. "We got a job to do."

While Horace ran toward the kitchen, Jasper headed upstairs. Nanny hurried after Jasper, yelling, "Don't you dare go up there, you big, long-legged lummox! I mean it!"

Nanny trotted into the first bedroom, and the door slammed behind her. She could hear Jasper laughing behind it. "You big weasel!" cried Nanny, realizing that she had been tricked.

Within minutes, it was over. Nanny heard Jasper calling down-

stairs, "Horace! Horace, me lad! I've got a sneakin' suspicion we're not welcome here. Pack up, we're leavin'."

Nanny yanked on the doorknob, but the door wouldn't budge. "Let me out!" she hollered. "Or I'll call the police!" Finally, the door flew open, and she ran downstairs.

"I'll bet they ran off with the good silver," she said to herself, hurrying into the kitchen. At first, everything seemed in place. Then she gasped. On the floor was an empty basket. Nanny grabbed a worn blanket in her hands, shouting, "The puppies! They took the puppies!"

Nanny ran into the dark street, searching for the police.

5

When Perdita and I returned to find the puppies gone, we were more than heartbroken. It was worse than if they had been sold, because we had no idea where they had been taken or what would happen to them. Perdita retreated to the kitchen, so I began to spend my days alone at the windowsill, wishing that the puppies would come bounding down the street.

News of the dognapping filled the papers. Anita and Roger waited by the phone, hoping someone would call to report that our puppies had been discovered. Roger suspected Cruella, but so far, no evidence against her had turned up.

One night, the phone jangled. Roger snatched it up. "Hello, inspector?" he inquired hopefully. But the person on the other end asked for Anita, and Roger handed the phone over.

"Hello, Cruella," said Anita. Both Roger and I glared. "Yes, it was quite a shock."

Roger whispered into Anita's ear, "What does she want? Is she calling to confess?"

Anita covered the mouthpiece with her hand. "Roger, please," she said. Then she returned to Cruella, saying, "Yes, we're doing everything we can. We've called Scotland Yard. But I'm afraid—"

Roger grabbed the phone from Anita. "Where are they? What have you done with them?"

Wincing, Anita took the phone and apologized to Cruella. "If there's any news, we'll let you know," she added before hanging up.

Then Anita turned to Roger. "I admit she's eccentric," she said, "but she's not a thief."

"She's still the number-one suspect in my book," maintained Roger, crossing his arms and puffing on his pipe.

"She's being investigated by Scotland Yard," Anita snapped. "What more do you want?"

When she saw the look of surprise on Roger's face, she leaned over and hugged him. "I'm sorry, Roger. But I don't know what to do. We've already thought of everything."

I hung my head and left the room, walking into the kitchen. I found Perdita lying on the floor beside the empty basket. She opened her eyes when I came in.

"Perdy, I'm afraid it's up to us," I said.

She stood up, frightened. "Pongo, isn't there any hope?"

"Yes. There's the Twilight Bark."

"The Twilight Bark?" she asked. "But dear, that's only a gossip chain."

"Perdy, it's the fastest way to send news," I told her. "If our puppies are anywhere in this city, the London dogs will know. We'll send the word tonight, when our pets take us for a walk in the park."

That evening, the icy ground chilled our feet and a bitter wind cut through our coats. With Anita and Roger, we stood on a hill overlooking London. I let out one long howl, then another. Perdita and I listened carefully for a response.

"There's no one out tonight," said Perdy. "I'm afraid it's too cold."

"We've got to keep trying, dear," I replied. I continued barking for several minutes, then stopped to listen. From very far away, there came a faint yelping.

"Perdy, we're in luck!" I said. "It's the Great Dane at Hampstead."

Tired of all our barking, Roger and Anita tugged at our leashes. Perdita and I refused to move, and I continued relaying my message.

Far away, in a yard, the Great Dane was straining to understand me. When a terrier next door heard the noise, he rushed out and began pestering him. "Who is it, Danny?" he asked.

"It's Pongo," replied the Great Dane. "He's calling from Regent's Park. It's an all-dog alert. Fifteen Dalmatian puppies have been stolen!"

"No!" cried the terrier. "Have they called Scotland Yard?"

Danny nodded, saying, "The humans have tried everything. Now it's up to us dogs—the Twilight Bark."

"I'll sound the alert," declared the terrier, and he barked so loudly and fiercely that he almost collapsed.

In a doghouse nearby, a Scotch terrier heard the message. Shocked, he relayed it through a drainpipe. The alert reached the Afghan I had seen in the park. She barked long and loud until some dogs in a pet shop heard her. From there, our desperate plea traveled to a fancy poodle, who leaped onto the top of a car and broadcast the news to the dogs in the street. The sound of a hundred howling dogs echoed across London, and I began to see lights blinking on as pets woke and tried to silence them.

The Twilight Bark reached the country, where a bloodhound named Towser heard it. He passed it on to the Colonel, an old English sheepdog. The Colonel got the message after a cat named Sergeant Tibs roused him from sleep.

"Now, look here, Tibs," groaned the sheepdog. "What's the idea of barging in at this hour of the night?"

"But Colonel—" Sergeant Tibs sputtered.

The sheepdog lifted a paw to silence him. "Hold on, Sergeant. Hear that? Sounds like an alert."

"Yes, Colonel, that's what I was trying to tell you."

"Well, we'd better look into it," declared the sheepdog. "Come along, Tibs. On the double."

"Yes, sir," said Sergeant Tibs, saluting. "Righto, sir."

They rushed to an open window to listen. A horse called Captain joined them. Both Captain and Sergeant Tibs watched the Colonel as he received the message in canine code.

"Sounds like a number," said the Colonel. "Three fives is thirteen."

"Ah, that's fifteen, sir," said Sergeant Tibs.

The Colonel nodded, and continued translating the message. "Dot . . . spot . . . ah, spotted . . . puddings, poodles . . . no, puddles. Fifteen spotted puddles stolen." Realizing that it didn't make sense, the Colonel shook his head in disgust. "Oh, balderdash!" he fumed.

Sergeant Tibs stood at attention. "Better double-check it, Colonel."

"Huh?" the Colonel asked, a bit confused. "Oh, yes, I suppose I had better." The Colonel began barking in code, hoping that Towser would hear him and repeat the message.

Moments later, the Colonel heard it. "Two woofs, one yip, and a woof."

Sergeant Tibs commented, "It sounds like 'puppies,' sir."

"Of course!" cried the Colonel. "Puppies!"

Saluting first, Sergeant Tibs reported, "Colonel! Colonel, sir. Two nights past, I heard puppies barking over at Hell Hall."

The Colonel raised an eyebrow. "You mean the old De Vil place? Nonsense, Tibs! No one's lived there for years."

Captain looked in the direction of the crumbling mansion. "Hold on," he said. "There's smoke coming from the chimney."

Surprised, the Colonel shook his head. "By Jove, that's strange," he said. "Strange indeed! I suppose we'd better investigate. I'll send word for old Towser to stand by."

After informing Towser, the Colonel and Sergeant Tibs made their way to Hell Hall. It looked as horrible as its name—a dark, gloomy mansion crowned with towers and turrets and surrounded by bare, gnarled trees.

"They say the old place is haunted, or some such fiddle-faddle," said the Colonel as he and Tibs stared through the gates.

"Ah, fiddle-faddle and rot, sir," Tibs replied bravely.

Nodding, the Colonel ordered Tibs to proceed. The cat gulped, then climbed up a tree whose branches overhung the wall. Leaping from limb to limb, he reached one of the mansion's upper-story windows and slipped inside.

The cat tiptoed down a hallway until he saw a sliver of light beneath a closed door. He couldn't open the door, but he saw a small hole in the wall and squeezed through it. Once inside, he was stunned

by what he saw. The room was full of Dalmatian puppies!

Sergeant Tibs peered around a chair. "Psst! Rover! Are you one of the fifteen stolen puppies?" he asked.

"No, I wasn't stolen," said the puppy. "I was bought and paid for. There are ninety-nine of us all together."

"Ninety-nine!" exclaimed the cat, rubbing his eyes in disbelief.

Another puppy had stirred and heard their conversation. She pointed to a group of puppies across the room, sitting in front of a television set. "How about that bunch of little ones? They have names and collars. They're not from a pet shop."

"I'd better count them," said Sergeant Tibs, as he headed in their direction.

"Watch out for the Baduns," warned the puppy.

"Baduns?" questioned Tibs. "Who are they?"

"Those two blokes, Horace and Jasper," said the puppy, pointing to two men lounging on a couch in front of the television. "They're awful mean."

Heeding the puppy's advice, Sergeant Tibs crawled along the floor until he reached the couch. He peeked around the side, knowing that at any moment one of the Baduns could whirl around and nab him.

Finally, when both Horace and Jasper were yelling at one of the puppies to get down from the television, Sergeant Tibs got an accurate count. There were fifteen puppies. As Tibs was about to sneak away to inform the Colonel, he felt a large hand grasp him by the neck. Jasper leered down at him. "Hey, Horace," he called, "how about a little cat casserole?"

Before the Baduns could devour him, Sergeant Tibs squirmed out of Jasper's grasp and dove for safety.

6

That night, while Perdita slept, I watched at the window, waiting for a response to the Twilight Bark. I had just about given up when I heard the great Dane howl from far across London. Someone had found our puppies! I woke Perdita, and we slipped out a bedroom window.

We met the great Dane at Primrose Hill, and he escorted us across the river. At Camden, he gave us directions. "When you reach Wither-marsh, contact old Towser," he said. "He'll direct you to the Colonel, who will take you to your puppies at the De Vil place."

"De Vil!" Perdita and I both exclaimed.

Perdita looked at me. "Oh, Pongo, it *was* her!" she said. "I hope we're not too late!"

After thanking the great Dane, we headed across the fields. Wither-marsh was miles away, and it would take us a long time to get there. On top of that, snow was beginning to fall. There was no question that it would slow our progress.

While the Colonel and Sergeant Tibs were waiting for us at the barn, they noticed a car drive up to Hell Hall. The Colonel became quite flustered. "Tibs! Tibs! Better see what's up!" he cried. "On the double, man! On the double!"

Leaving Captain in charge, the Colonel and Sergeant Tibs hurried toward Hell Hall. Once Sergeant Tibs was inside, he raced to the

hole in the wall. He peered inside and saw Cruella pacing the room, ranting at Horace and Jasper. "I've got no time to argue," she insisted. "It's got to be done tonight. Do you understand? Tonight!"

"But they ain't big enough," Horace whined.

"Yeah," agreed Jasper. "You couldn't get a dozen coats out of the whole caboodle."

Sergeant Tibs blinked in amazement. Cruella was planning to make dog-skin coats!

"We'll have to settle for half a dozen," she was shouting. "We can't wait—the police are everywhere. I want the job done tonight!"

"How are we going to do it?" asked Horace.

"Any way you like!" Cruella screamed. "Poison them, drown them,

bash their heads in! I don't care how you kill the little beasts, but do it. And do it now!" Behind her, the puppies trembled in fear.

Jasper didn't give them a glance. He was more interested in the television. "Please, miss," he begged Cruella, "have pity, will you? Can't we see the rest of our show first?"

Enraged, Cruella grabbed a bottle and threw it into the fireplace. As it shattered against the bricks, the puppies scrambled to hide behind furniture and boxes. Shuddering, Sergeant Tibs watched from his place at the wall.

"Now listen, you idiots!" Cruella ordered the Baduns. "I'll be back in the morning. If the job isn't done by then, I'll call the police! You wouldn't want to go back to jail, would you? Would you?"

Cruella slammed the door behind her, and the entire mansion shook. Plaster fell from the ceiling, raining down on Sergeant Tibs as he scampered into the room. He hurried over to the puppies. "Hey, kids," he said, "you'd better get out of here if you want to save your skins."

"But how?" asked one of the pups.

"Shh!" cautioned Sergeant Tibs. "There's a hole in the wall, by the door. Come on. Follow me."

As Jasper and Horace stared at the television set, Sergeant Tibs led all the puppies toward the hole. The little ones tumbled all over one another as Tibs tried to make them stay in a straight line. "One at at a time," he whispered. "Climb through one at a time."

As the show wound to a close, Sergeant Tibs tried to hurry the remaining puppies. "Come on, snap it up!" he urged. "Faster! Faster!"

Rolly was the last in line, and just as Tibs was about to push him through, the cat glanced at the television set. There was Lucky, staring at the screen!

Sergeant Tibs crawled past the feet of Horace and Jasper. "Hey, kid," the cat whispered, "let's go." The television was so loud that Lucky didn't hear him. Sergeant Tibs reached out to grab the puppy, but Horace beat him to it.

"Get out of the way, you little runt," snarled Horace, shoving the puppy aside. Sergeant Tibs snatched Lucky up and carried him away. When they reached the hole in the wall, Rolly was still waiting. He let Lucky climb through first, but when Rolly took his turn, the ever-hungry puppy got stuck.

As Sergeant Tibs struggled to push Rolly into the hall, he heard Jasper shout, "Horace, look! They're gone!"

Using all his strength, Sergeant Tibs shoved Rolly through the hole. He ordered all the puppies to hurry down the stairs. Behind him, Jasper was calling, "Here, puppies! Don't go hidin' from your old Uncle Jasper. I'm not going to hurt you. Come out, wherever you are."

Sergeant Tibs hid the puppies under the staircase. "Here they come," he whispered. "Don't breathe a word."

Jasper stomped down the steps, shining a flashlight around the dark mansion. "Double-crossin' little twerps," he muttered to Horace, "pullin' a snitch on us. And after we took care of 'em all this time. There's gratitude for you."

"It ain't fair, Jasper," agreed Horace.

As the Baduns were talking, Rolly poked his head out of hiding. Sergeant Tibs grabbed Rolly to pull him back, and the puppy squealed. Jasper shone the flashlight in their direction. "Hey, Horace," Jasper cried, "I found 'em!"

The chase was on. Sergeant Tibs led the puppies down a hall, past a window where the Colonel was looking in. Remembering his duty, Tibs cried, "Sorry, sir. Can't stop now. No time to explain. Busy, sir."

Sergeant Tibs and his charges rushed into a large room. The Baduns burst in, slamming the door behind them. Sergeant Tibs and the puppies were trapped.

7

After traveling for hours across icy fields and wading through cold, rushing rivers, Perdita and I discovered that we were lost. We were approaching a run-down mansion, hoping to find someone who could help us. It was then that I heard the barking.

We bounded through the snow toward the sound. When I saw an old English sheepdog buried up to his whiskers, I cried, "Colonel? Are you the Colonel?"

"Pongo? You must be Pongo!" the sheepdog exclaimed.

Perdita didn't take time to introduce herself. "Our puppies!" she blurted. "Are they all right?"

"I'm afraid there's trouble," said the Colonel. "Big hullabaloo at the house. Come along quickly!"

We followed the Colonel to a window. When I looked in, I saw the puppies first, then Jasper looming over them with a fireplace poker in his hand. Sergeant Tibs was trying his best to protect them.

"Perdita, look!" I cried. A moment later, we crashed through the window, shattering the glass. We advanced toward Jasper and Horace, growling fiercely.

"What have we here?" sneered Jasper. "A pair of spotted hyenas?" He backed up, pretending not to be afraid. Then he shoved his brother in our direction. "Come on, old pal, get 'em."

Horace waved a chair leg at Perdita, so I lunged at him, grabbing
the stick in my mouth. Horace grabbed it away from me, and when
his arm jerked backward, he hit Jasper on the head. His brother
slumped in pain. Then Jasper went after Horace, kicking him in the
seat of the pants. Throughout the fight, the puppies barked wildly.

It wasn't over. Perdita tore at Jasper's pant leg, and he grabbed a
chair to defend himself. Before Jasper brought it down on Perdy's
head, I lunged at him. The chair flew out of his hands. Jasper kicked
me, and I went sailing backward, slamming into the door. I had
barely recovered when Jasper rushed at me with the poker. I slipped
between his legs and escaped.

During the battle, Sergeant Tibs had begun leading the puppies toward safety. The Colonel stood at the sidelines, calling, "Retreat! Retreat!"

In the meantime, Perdy had managed to pull a coat over Horace's head, confusing him. "Jasper! Jasper!" Horace cried. "Get me out of here!" He stumbled and fell into the fireplace, landing in the flames. When Horace jumped up, he accidentally knocked Jasper into the wall. More plaster came crashing down, this time on top of the Baduns.

"Come on, Perdy," I shouted. "Let's go!" We raced out of the house after the puppies.

Once we had arrived safely at the barn, the puppies began leaping on us and shouting, "Dad! Mother! Dad! We sure missed you, Mother! Here we are, Dad!"

Perdy tried to hug each puppy. "My darlings!" she murmured. "Oh, my darlings!"

Rolly jumped on my back. "Did you bring me anything to eat, Dad?" he asked, and I laughed.

"Is everybody here?" I questioned them. "All fifteen?"

Patch gazed up at me. "We have twice that many now," he said. "There's ninety-nine of us."

"What?" I exclaimed. "Ninety-nine? But where did the others come from?"

Perdy and I surveyed the mob of squirming puppies. "What on earth would that devil woman want with so many?" asked Perdita.

One of the pet-store puppies answered, "She was going to make coats out of us."

"No! She wouldn't!" exclaimed Perdita.

Sergeant Tibs nodded. "That's right. Dog-skin coats."

"Dog-skin coats?" asked the Colonel, frowning. "Come now, Tibs. That's not possible."

"But it's true, sir!" insisted the cat.

Patch chimed in, jumping up and down excitedly. "Horace and Jasper were going to pop us off and . . . and skin us!"

"She's a devil!" Perdy repeated. "A witch! What will we do?"

There was only one answer. "We have to get back to London somehow," I said.

Patch looked at his new friends and said, "What about the others? What will they do?"

"We'll take them home with us," I decided instantly. "All of them! Our pets would never turn them out."

Just then, Captain addressed the Colonel. "Lights on the road, sir. It's a truck heading this way."

Sergeant Tibs stood at attention. "It's Horace and Jasper. They followed our tracks."

"We've got them outnumbered, Tibs," said the Colonel. "When I give the signal, we'll attack."

Sergeant Tibs saluted respectfully and replied, "Colonel, sir, I'm afraid that would be disastrous, sir."

"He's right, Colonel," I said. "We'd better run for it."

Sergeant Tibs suggested that we take the back way, across the

pasture. "Thank you all," I said sincerely. "How can we ever repay you?"

The Colonel cleared his throat, happy and embarrassed. "Not at all. All in the line of duty!"

"That's right, sir," Sergeant Tibs said. "Routine!"

We heard the truck pull in at the gate. Perdy led the puppies outside, urging them to hurry.

"Good luck to all of you!" cried Captain.

"Good luck!" added the Colonel. "And never fear. We'll hold them off to the bitter end."

The Colonel was true to his word. As Perdy ushered the puppies out of the barn, the Colonel and his men confronted Horace and Jasper. They fought them off until Perdy and I could get all ninety-nine puppies to safety. However, with the snow, it was impossible to cover our tracks. I knew it would be only a matter of time before the Baduns found us.

Perdita and I hurried through the snow with the puppies, trying to make sure that no one got lost. The puppies were too tired to complain, so they followed obediently. Occasionally, one would slip and fall, and either Perdy or I would come to the rescue, nudging the puppy onto its feet.

As we crossed a road, I heard a truck rattle behind us. With Perdita's help, I herded the puppies under a bridge. We huddled together, holding our breath.

The truck stopped above us. A flashlight shone through the trees. I heard Jasper say, "They've got to be around here somewhere."

"Jasper, I've been thinkin'," announced Horace.

"Now, Horace, didn't I warn you about thinkin'?"

Ignoring Jasper's comment, Horace beamed the flashlight across the ice and said, "What if the dogs went down the frozen creek, so they wouldn't leave any tracks?"

Jasper stared at his brother. "You idiot!" he shouted, grabbing Horace's arm. "Dogs ain't that smart!"

As soon as they drove off, we headed down the frozen stream. We did our best to move quickly without falling. Patch cried, "We gave 'em the slip, didn't we, Dad?"

"They didn't even see us, Patch," declared Penny before I could answer.

"Shh, children! Shh!" Perdy reminded them.

The puppies had a hard time trying to stay on all fours. They kept slipping and sliding, until one had the idea of grabbing onto Perdita's tail and letting her drag him along. The other puppies gripped one another's tails to form a line, but a few at the back slid into one another.

"My feet are slippery," said Patch.

"I wish we could walk on snow," added Lucky.

"No, son," I told him. "We can't leave tracks."

By the next morning, the puppies became tired of trudging through the wet and cold. I had to keep counting them for fear that one would give up and refuse to travel any farther. As our group climbed a hill, Lucky did just that. He plopped down and let the falling snow settle on his coat.

"Come on, Lucky," I urged him. "We can't give up now."

"I'm tired, and I'm hungry, and my tail is froze," whimpered Lucky. "And my nose is froze. And my ears are froze. And my toes are froze!"

As I picked him up, wondering how I would carry more than one tired pup, a collie came running toward us. He was the first dog we had seen since leaving the barn.

"Pongo!" he cried. "We'd almost given up hope. We have shelter for you at the dairy farm across the road."

I left Lucky with the collie and ran to the front of the line. "Perdy! Perdy!" I cried. "This way!"

With the wind blowing their ears back, the puppies turned and headed for the dairy. They filed inside, shivering and exhausted.

Inside the dairy were three cows. As the puppies settled into the straw, the one named Queenie said, "We were so worried about you! How did you make it all this way? And in such dreadful weather!"

Before I could answer, Rolly crawled over to Perdita. "I'm hungry, Mother. I'm hungry."

The other puppies took up the cry. Perdita gazed down at them sadly. "I'm sorry, children," she sighed.

As Perdy and I urged the puppies to get some sleep, the cows whispered among themselves. Then Queenie asked, "Do they like warm milk? It's fresh."

Rolly sat up. "Where is it? Where is it?"

Queenie grinned. "Come and get it, kids. It's on the house!"

The puppies gathered around the cows and drank as much milk as their little stomachs could handle. As Perdy and I thanked the cows for their generosity, the collie returned with some meat scraps.

"It's not much," the collie said, "but it might hold you as far as Dinsford. There's a Labrador retriever there whose pet is a grocer."

Perdy and I looked at each other. Dinsford seemed far away, and London even farther. Yet we had to keep going if we were ever going to be reunited with our pets.

"Get some rest," the collie continued, "and try not to worry. I'll stand watch."

The next morning, we continued our journey across the country-side. As we crossed a muddy road, I heard a car honking. "Hurry, kids! Hurry!" I cried, guiding them into the woods. I grabbed a tree branch and swept the snow behind us, trying to erase our tracks. I raced after Perdita and the puppies just as the car screeched to a halt.

Peering around a tree, I saw Cruella back up and examine the snow beside the road. She pounded on the horn until Jasper and Horace drove up in their truck. After a brief conversation, they headed in different directions. I prayed that we would reach Dinsford before they did.

As soon as we made it into town, the Labrador met us. "Pongo!" he cried. "I've got a ride home for you. Follow me."

The Labrador guided us into an old blacksmith's shop. After Perdy and I told the puppies to remain quiet, the Labrador led us to a window and pointed to a truck parked down the street. "That furniture van is going to London as soon as the engine's repaired," he said. "There'll be room for all of you."

"Pongo!" interrupted Perdita. "There's Cruella!"

Her roadster paused by the van, then slowly headed toward us. We ducked down as Cruella drove by. After she had passed the shop, I peeked through the window and saw Jasper and Horace. They were hurrying down the street on foot, searching for us.

"Oh, Pongo!" whispered Perdita. "How will we get to the van?"

"I don't know, Perdy," I answered. "But somehow, we've got to find a way." I looked at the puppies and wondered how in the world we would ever escape.

As Perdita and I tried to form a plan, two of the puppies began arguing. Lucky ran over to us, half covered in soot. "Dad, Patch pushed me into the fireplace," he complained.

As I was about to scold them, I was stopped by the sight of Lucky's blackened coat. "Perdy, I have an idea!" I cried. Then I jumped into the fireplace and rolled in the soot, doing all I could to disguise my spotted coat.

"Look! I'm a Labrador!" I called to Perdita after I stood up. The puppies stared at me, startled.

"We'll all roll in the soot," I cried. "We'll all be Labradors! Cruella will never recognize us then." I turned to the puppies and said, "Come on, kids, roll in the soot."

"You mean you *want* us to get dirty?" asked Penny.

"Mother, should we?" wondered Patch.

"Do as your father says," Perdita answered, nodding.

"This'll be fun," cried one of the store-bought pups. "I always wanted to get good and dirty!"

The puppies giggled as they rolled over and over in the soot. "That's right!" I cried. "The dirtier the better!"

The Dinsford Labrador gathered the puppies near a hole in the wall and told them to wait. When he peeked out, he saw Horace and

Jasper entering a store across the street. He waited until they were inside, then led the first group of puppies to the van.

As the Labrador was loading them into the back, I told Perdita, "So far so good. Come on, Perdy. You'd better put on your makeup."

After I left, I heard Cruella's car rattling down the street, then saw Jasper and Horace approach the shop window. They would have seen Perdita if Cruella hadn't distracted them, shrieking, "Jasper! Horace! Where are those puppies?"

"Be reasonable, miss," pleaded Jasper. "We're frozen clean to our bones. We haven't had a bite to eat all day."

Cruella banged her fist on the side of her car. "They're somewhere in this village," she screamed, "and we're going to find them! Now get going!"

I quickly helped the Labrador load a bunch of puppies into the van, then ran back for Perdita. I heard the driver warming up the engine. "Hurry, Perdy!" I called. "The van's about to leave."

Perdita rushed out with another batch of puppies. Their coats shone black against the snow. I gathered another group and headed toward the van. As we were scampering across the street, Cruella returned. Perdy ran back for another bunch of puppies. As she passed me, I told her I'd get the rest.

By this time, Horace and Jasper had decided to search the blacksmith's shop. When they failed to find an entrance along the street, they hurried around to the back. It was my only chance to get the last group out safely. "Hurry, kids!" I cried, knowing that the Baduns would enter at any second. I nudged the last bunch of puppies into the snow.

Cruella's car sputtered in our direction. She stopped in front of us and leaned out the window, staring intently at the black puppies. Lucky leaned against my leg, shivering at the sight of her. "She's catching us, Dad," he whimpered.

"Keep going! Keep going!" I muttered under my breath.

As the last few puppies made it out of the shop, drops of melting snow fell from the eaves. Horrified, I watched white spots appear on the puppies' coats where the water washed off the soot. I pushed the puppies along, well aware that Cruella was spying on us. She grinned when a large clump of snow fell on Lucky, burying him. As I hastily pulled him out with my teeth, I saw that he had been washed clean

of the soot. Every spot stood out against his white coat.

"Horace! Jasper!" Cruella yelled. "They're trying to escape in the van! After them!"

As I grabbed Lucky and raced to the van, the Baduns hurried around the shop. I slipped once, but managed to get up and leap on the back of the van as it sped away. After tossing Lucky to Perdita, I clung to the tailgate with my toenails. Behind me, I could hear the Labrador barking as he scuffled with the Baduns.

Finally I was able to pull myself up into the back of the van. I was happy to see the puppies settling themselves in boxes and drawers as the van rumbled down the road.

"Pongo!" cried Perdy, pointing. "There's Cruella!"

The roadster zoomed toward us. Cruella steered alongside the van, trying to force it off the road. The driver tried desperately to avoid being forced off a cliff. "Hey, lady!" he shouted. "What in thunder are you trying to do?"

Again, Cruella tried to pass the van. It veered to the side, bouncing puppies out of the drawers. The driver was trying mightily to keep the truck upright, and he succeeded.

As Cruella drove alongside the van, trying to bash it in the side, a one-lane bridge loomed before us. The van made it onto the bridge, but Cruella crashed through a barricade. She bounced into the gully and became stuck in a snowbank. The van made it across the bridge and continued on the road.

"Pongo, look!" cried Perdita, pointing up a hill. The Baduns' truck barreled toward us. The next moment, Cruella appeared behind us in her roadster, which she had managed to free from the snow. With a wild look in her eyes, she rammed her car into the back of the van, shoving it forward. Perdita and I flew against the side as Cruella yanked her steering wheel toward the left, trying to stop both vehicles.

Looking around the side of the van, I saw Jasper's truck roaring down on us, spinning out of control. I watched it collide with Cruella's car. Both vehicles were knocked away from the van. The truck and the roadster flew into the air. When they came to earth, they shattered into pieces, the debris littering the snowdrifts.

I looked out of the back of the van to see Cruella emerge from the wreckage, waving her fist at the Baduns. I was delighted to see that the fur coat she was wearing had been torn to shreds, and to know that she would not have another one for a long time . . . as long as justice was done, and Cruella was put in jail.

When the van finally made it to London, we were a tired and dirty lot. Our fifteen puppies hopped out of the van, happy to see the Radcliff home again. The other eighty-four pups seemed shy at first, but then they gathered up their courage and followed me and Perdita to the door.

I peeked into the window before announcing our arrival. It seemed as though Anita was trying to cheer up Roger, who was slumped in a chair. As he examined the photograph that Cruella De Vil had admired long ago, Nanny entered the room, wiping away a tear.

I couldn't let Nanny think the worst for another moment. I began barking, softly at first, but soon as loud as my lungs would allow.

The door was flung open. I bounded in, heading straight for Roger. His mouth dropped in surprise as I jumped on him and knocked him over. As I hurried to greet Nanny, Perdita leaped into the room, followed by the puppies. Anita cried, "What on earth?"

"Why, they're Labradors!" exclaimed Roger. I had forgotten that our coats were still black!

Nanny looked at the paw marks I had made on her white apron. "No, they're covered with soot!" she shouted joyfully. "Look, here's Lucky! He's the only one with his spots!"

Roger pulled out his handkerchief and wiped my face. "Oh, Pongo!

Is that you?" he asked, grinning. "It's Pongo!"

Anita cleaned Perdita's face with her apron and said, "And it's Perdy! My darling!"

Nanny grabbed a broom and began gently sweeping soot off the puppies. "It's Patch, and Rolly, and Penny! They're all here, the little dears." Nanny gazed around the room, puzzled at first. "And look, there's a whole lot more!"

"Anita, there are puppies everywhere!" cried Roger, noticing that every rug, every chair, every step of the stairs was covered with puppies. They began counting, and you can imagine their surprise when they came up with a total of ninety-nine. Adding me and Perdita, that made one hundred and one Dalmatians!

"Where did they all come from?" asked Anita.

Roger scratched me under the neck. "Pongo, you old rascal!"

At the thought of so many puppies, Anita almost fainted. "What will we do with them?" she asked Roger.

"We'll keep them!" Roger proclaimed. "We'll buy a big place in the country, and we'll have a plantation! A Dalmatian plantation!"

Roger hurried to the piano and began improvising a song. While we had been searching for the puppies, he had written a song about Cruella, that was to become his first hit! As he pounded out the chords to his new tune, all the puppies began barking. Perdita and I joined in, and soon the house was ringing with the voices of one hundred and one Dalmatians!